The illustrations in this book were made
with watercolor on paper.

Cataloging-in-Publication Data has been
applied for and may be obtained from the Library of Congress.
ISBN 978-0-8109-8412-7

Book design by Chad W. Beckerman

Printed and bound in China
10 9 8 7 6 5 4 3 2 1

Abrams Books for Young Readers are available at special dis-
counts when purchased in quantity for premiums and promotions
as well as fundraising or educational use. Special editions can also
be created to specification. For details, contact specialmarkets@
abramsbooks.com or the address below.

ABRAMS
THE ART OF BOOKS SINCE 1949

115 West 18th Street
New York, NY 10011
www.abramsbooks.com

For Lois and Lee, for their
support and friendship
—L.N.

For teachers and librarians everywhere—thank you
for all the wonderful work you do
—N.E.

For Diana
—L.M.

Anna loved to read.

She read while grocery shopping with her dad.

She read while jumping rope.

And she even read while taking a bubble bath.

After school each day, Anna rushed to the library to
return the books she had finished and look for new ones.

There was nothing more exciting
than finding a good book!

After the library, Anna met her
best friends, Emily, Nicole, and Bitsy.

Emily loved to dance,

Nicole loved to play soccer,

and Bitsy loved to paint.

Their favorite place was Petunia's, where they loved to share their favorite candy—jellybeans!

Just as jellybeans are different flavors but go well together, the girls were all different but got along great—and so they called themselves the Jellybeans!

The next day at school, homework was assigned. They had to go to the library, read a book about something they loved, and write a report on it. The class was going to have a Book Bonanza!

Anna was thrilled! Now she could take the Jellybeans to the library with her.

The Jellybeans met the librarian,
Ms. Beasley-Buzzer. She always knew
how to help with finding good books.

"Hi, Anna," Ms. Beasley-Buzzer said. "Are these your friends?"

"Yes," Anna answered shyly. "We're here to do book reports."

"I'd rather be dancing," Emily said.

"I wish I was playing soccer," Nicole added.

"When can I go paint?" Bitsy asked.

Anna said quietly to her friends, "Just as jellybeans come in lots of flavors, there's a book that everyone will like."

"Anna's right," Ms. Beasley-Buzzer said. "I think we can find the right book for each of you."

Ms. Beasley-Buzzer showed Emily where the books on dancing were.

Emily found a beautiful book on ballet.

Then Ms. Beasley-Buzzer helped Nicole find a book about soccer.

And Bitsy found a book about famous painters.

The girls sat down to read. They were excited to find the perfect books.

But Anna still needed to find one.

"Follow me, Anna," Ms. Beasley-Buzzer said. "I have
a brand-new book that might be just right."

Anna smiled when she saw the big book of fairy tales. As she read it, she imagined herself as one of the princesses in the book. Now she was ready to write her report.

The next day, the students read their
reports in front of the class.

When it was Anna's turn, she couldn't get up!

"What's wrong?" Emily whispered.

"I read by myself every day," Anna whispered,
"but I'm scared to read aloud in front of the class."

"We'll help you," Nicole said.

"It will be great," Bitsy added.

"I know you can do it!" Emily said.

The Jellybeans went up to the front of the class and held hands. Anna started to read very slowly.

"Reading is the most magical thing in the world," Anna said quietly. "That's why I chose this book on fairy tales."

She still couldn't look up at the class.

"Keep going!" the Jellybeans said.

"I love to read because I can go anywhere or be anything in a book," Anna said with excitement.

"Like a ballerina. Or a soccer star. Or a famous artist. Or even a fairy tale-reading princess!"

The class applauded. The girls gave Anna a big hug.

"That was a great report!" Nicole said.

"I never knew reading could be so much fun," Bitsy added.

"I was so nervous," said Anna. "I couldn't have done it without you."

"Let's go celebrate!" Emily said.

"I know the perfect place," Anna said.

And so they went to Petunia's for their favorite candy . . .